Bristol & Somerset

Edited By Catherine Cook

First published in Great Britain in 2019 by:

Young Writers
Remus House
Coltsfoot Drive
Peterborough
PE2 9BF
Telephone: 01733 890066
Website: www.youngwriters.co.uk

All Rights Reserved
Book Design by Spencer Hart
© Copyright Contributors 2019
Softback ISBN 978-1-78988-997-0
Hardback ISBN 978-1-78988-998-7
Printed and bound in the UK by BookPrintingUK
Website: www.bookprintinguk.com
YB0419P

Foreword

Dear Reader,

Are you ready to explore the wonderful delights of poetry?

Young Writers' *Poetry Patrol* gang set out to encourage and ignite the imaginations of 5-7 year-olds as they took their first steps into the magical world of poetry. With **Riddling Rabbit**, **Acrostic Croc** and **Sensory Skunk** on hand to help, children were invited to write an acrostic, sense poem or riddle on any theme, from people to places, animals to objects, food to seasons. *Poetry Patrol* is also a great way to introduce children to the use of poetic expression, including onomatopoeia and similes, repetition and metaphors, acting as stepping stones for their future poetic journey.

All of us here at Young Writers believe in the importance of inspiring young children to produce creative writing, including poetry, and we feel that seeing their own poem in print will keep that creative spirit burning brightly and proudly.

We hope you enjoy reading this wonderful collection as much as we enjoyed reading all the entries.

Contents

St Aldhelm's CE (VA) Primary School, Doulting

Lily Hoddinott (8)	53
Corey Lincoln (8)	54
Oliver Harris (7)	55
Fabio Knott (8)	56
Grant Jeffery (8)	57
Harry Bassett (8)	58
Sienna Oakman (7)	59
Alfie Beachcroft (8)	60
Lola Gregory (7)	61
Owen Pitman (8)	62

St John's CE Primary School, Midsomer Norton

Nikita Fisher (6)	63
Alicia Hurst (6)	64
Isla Seymour (6)	65
Isla Miles (6)	66
Ethan Simcox (6)	67
Isaac Brooks (6)	68
Hannah Evans (6)	69
James Parry (6)	70
Freddie Maule (6)	71
Sophia Perry (6)	72
Taylor Rose Hampson (7)	73
Poppy-Lou Tustin (6)	74
Joshua Anderson (6)	75

St Nicholas CE Primary School, Henstridge

Alfie Cochrane (7)	76
Ronnie Smith (7)	77
Ryan Shearing (7)	78
Archie Craig (7)	79
Izabella Shearer (6)	80
Amy Cluett (7)	81
Daniel Furlong (6)	82
Ella Frampton	83
Zachary Peckover (6)	84
Shane Cherrington (6)	85

Courtney-Mae Read (6)	86
Jessica Squires (6)	87
Finn Jameson (5)	88
Kaydie Cherrington (7)	89

Sunny Hill Preparatory School, Bruton

Cecily Gasson-Hargreaves (5)	90
Jamie Stean (7)	91
Isabelle Kettle (6)	92
Tabitha Bayliss (6)	93
Nina Markussdottir (5)	94
Rose Ward (6)	95
Rose Turner (5)	96

The Dolphin School, Bristol

Coco Green (6)	97
Martha Eldred (7)	98
Eliza Jane Postema (7)	99
Farris Shandis (7)	100
Aki Maxwell (7)	101
Alina Kabir (7)	102
Ashley-Joseph Dymond-Bailey (7)	103
Eshaal Fatima Shakeel (7)	104
Leen Elmouiz Siddeg Hessien (6)	105
Umamah Hassan (7)	106
Ahmed Mohamed (7)	107
Suhana Gill (7)	108
Isra Ismail (7)	109
Annaliese Smith (7)	110
Amelie Papworth Jory (7)	111
Myar Khalil	112
Zakoni Barrington Alcott-Kennett (7)	113
Nehal Sunu (6)	114
Owen Taylor (7)	115
Kenneth Oommen Panicker (7)	116
Bushra Ahmed (7)	117

The Poems

RIDDLIN' RABBIT

SENSORY SKUNK

ACROSTIC CROC

My Guinea Pigs

G uinea pigs, guinea pigs, my furry friends.
U p through the tunnel, the fun never ends.
I always like to hear them squeak.
N ever get bored of a sneaky peek.
E very day I have to check they have plenty for munching.
A lways lots of carrots crunching.

P iggies are playful and kind.
I always have them on my mind.
G uinea pigs, guinea pigs, my furry friends.
S o glad I have them, the fun never ends.

Emily Lawrence (6)
Bishop Henderson CE Primary School, Taunton

All The Parts Of A Creepy Dragon

Dragons have spiky claws that could kill you.
Dragons have long tails that are wavy and very strong.
Dragons have burning flames that can burn almost everything, even you.
Dragons have pointy teeth that, if you touch, you will die.
Dragons have scaly bodies that could scare you.
Dragons have creepy eyes that could hypnotise you.
Dragons have slimy tongues that will make you go *yuck!*
Dragons have poisoned horns that you'll run away from.
Dragons have giant wings which are super wavy.

Dragons have giant tummies that will make you scream.
Those are the amazing things of a creepy dragon.

Jophiel Joice Philip (7)
Bishop Henderson CE Primary School, Taunton

The Brilliant Beach

At the beach, I see beautiful, colourful shells in the rock pools and the sand.
At the beach, I hear the waves crashing together, I hear seagulls squawking and children running around.
At the beach, I taste ice cream with chocolate flakes. Yum!
At the beach, I feel chilly, cold water under my toes, soft sand on my hand and bumpy rocks in the rockpools.
At the beach, I smell hot fish and chips and suncream on my skin.
I love the beach and I can't wait to go again.

Toby Russell (5)
Bishop Henderson CE Primary School, Taunton

I Love Butterflies

B eautiful pattern on its wings.
U tterly lovely colours.
T hey have to have wings to fly.
T wirling in the sky.
E very one of them dancing.
R eady to collect its nectar.
F luttering around the flowers.
L ittle antennae smelling.
Y ellow, pink and blue, all different colours.

Florence Needham (6)

Bishop Henderson CE Primary School, Taunton

Summer's Day

A summer's day smells like freshly cut grass
and barbecues.
A summer's day tastes like ice cream.
A summer's day looks like butterflies
and picnics.
A summer's day feels warm and fuzzy.
A summer's day sounds like birds chirping
and children playing.

Imogen Collins (6)

Bishop Henderson CE Primary School, Taunton

The Magical Unicorn

The magical unicorn smells like blossoms.
The magical unicorn feels as soft as snow.
The magical unicorn is pretty, with a golden horn and feathery wings.
The magical unicorn sounds like sparkles in the air.
The magical unicorn reminds me of wishes.

Martha Wright (6)
Bishop Henderson CE Primary School, Taunton

I Can Fly In The Sky

I can fly with my blue and pink fluffy wings.
I give good children money and sweet dreams.
I only fly at night.
During the day I make my castle with the teeth I collect from children.
Who am I?

Answer: *The tooth fairy.*

Rosie Date (6)
Bishop Henderson CE Primary School, Taunton

Castles

C astles have thick walls.

A ll castles have knights.

S ome castles are attacked.

T oday you can see castles in ruins.

L ots of castles have baileys.

E very castle has a keep.

Sebastian Hemmings (6)

Bishop Henderson CE Primary School, Taunton

Rosie The Butterfly

I like to fly and look for flowers.
I live in Jessica's garden.
I like to eat the sweet nectar.
I love bright colours and pretty flowers.
I have big beautiful wings and antennae.
I am Rosie, the butterfly.

Jessica Tilleray (6)
Bishop Henderson CE Primary School, Taunton

Woods

W onderful animals in the woods.

O h, how scary it is when it's dark.

O h, how colourful it is when it's light.

D arkness falls and wolves come out.

S lithering goes the snake.

Sophie Keeble (7)

Bishop Henderson CE Primary School, Taunton

My Bunny

B ig floppy ears.

U sually hops about.

N ibbles on carrots.

N ice to cuddle.

Y ou might have a bunny too.

Gabriella Lawton (7)
Bishop Henderson CE Primary School, Taunton

An Amazing Summer

S ummer is really great.

U nless it rains all summer.

M aybe you will have an ice cream.

M aybe you will go to the beach.

E very summer is nice, even if it rains.

R ainbows might come.

Elicie Savage (6)

Emersons Green Primary School, Emersons Green

Adventures Around The World

A melia Earhart flying in the sky.

D oing amazing things.

V ile people can make traps

E ntertainment for people.

N ot good for people who didn't believe in them.

T rying not to die.

U nfair lives.

R eally bad weather.

E asy learning.

R eally hard training.

S winging through vines.

Tashi Fujiwara-Nandy (7)
Fishponds CE Academy, Fishponds

Under The Sea!

U nder the sea

N emo swims through the coral

D ark green seaweed

E nding a dive

R edoing the dive

T raining your diving

H iding fish in the coral

E els, which are garden eels, sleeping in the sand

S harks biting fish

E lectric eels swimming

A nchors from ships.

Nikodem Dabski (6)
Fishponds CE Academy, Fishponds

Pokémon

P okémon and their trainer Ash.

O peration Pokémon battle.

K atie and Ash always work together.

E ntertaining people at Pokémon school.

M aster Ash always taking challenges.

O pponents want to steal Pikachu.

N avigating through Pokémon world is always helpful.

Benjamin Oladipupo (7)

Fishponds CE Academy, Fishponds

Pokémon

P oké Balls.

O peration Pokémon battle.

K atie and Ash are best friends.

E ntertaining people to learn about Pokémon.

M aster Ash is a good Pokémon trainer.

O pponents against Ash always want to win.

N ever tease a wild Pokémon.

Jack Duncan Ross (7)
Fishponds CE Academy, Fishponds

The Beach!

T he beach feels like sandy toes
H ummingbirds humming all day
E xciting waves splashing

B eautiful sights
E agles eating yummy fish
A warm glow
C rackling hot sand
H ope you have a lovely time.

Mobolajoko Abigael Olanibijuwon (6)
Fishponds CE Academy, Fishponds

Jurassic World

Dinosaurs smell like green goop.
Dinosaurs look like green goop robots.
Dinosaurs lived over a thousand years ago.
Cavemen lived at the same time as
dinosaurs.
They were afraid of each other.
Dinosaurs were afraid of other dinosaurs.
Some dinosaurs have spikes.

Yuvraj Singh Sandhu (6)
Fishponds CE Academy, Fishponds

Springtime

S weet-smelling blossom.

P retty flowers swaying in the wind.

R obins pecking in the dirt.

I nsects running all around.

N ests being built high in trees.

G rass swaying in the wind.

Sylvia Weston (7)

Fishponds CE Academy, Fishponds

December Fun

D ying leaves.

E ating roast dinner.

C hristmas is nearly here.

E verlasting fun.

M erry holiday.

B eautiful toys.

E vergreen trees.

R oaring flames dancing.

Beatrice Prudence Fliski-Kingsbury (7)
Fishponds CE Academy, Fishponds

Seaside

S easide.

E cosystem from whales.

A t the seaside people are relaxing.

S eas are all wavy.

I 'd rather stay at the seaside.

D rinking fizzy pop.

E ating tasty food.

Toni Filipov (6)

Fishponds CE Academy, Fishponds

Spring Blossoms!

B lossom is beautiful.

L ovely and pink.

O ften found in spring.

S o many colours.

S pring is filled with them.

O ur world is full of them.

M agnificent flowers.

Elsie Wood (7)
Fishponds CE Academy, Fishponds

Winter Is Fun

Winter smells like a cold feeling in your heart.
Winter looks like frosty clouds.
Winter sounds like robins chirping.
Winter feels like hot chocolate.
Winter tastes like steaming soup.

Nafisa Ali (6)
Fishponds CE Academy, Fishponds

Spring

S unshine.

P erfect nature.

R abbits hiding in their holes.

I nside because in spring it might rain.

N ests are in nature.

G reat fun times.

Jessica Dury (5)
Fishponds CE Academy, Fishponds

Summer

Summer smells like sizzling barbecues.
Summer looks like a really hot country.
Summer tastes like flowers.
Summer sounds like playing in the sea.
Summer feels like super hot sand.

Ruby Chandler (6)

Fishponds CE Academy, Fishponds

Rabbits

Running fast
Looks good
Bouncing bunnies
Feels bouncy
Bunnies feel soft
I love rabbits
They are soft
Their teeth stick out!

Aishie Sharif (6)
Fishponds CE Academy, Fishponds

The Sea

The waves are high.
The sea tastes salty.
The sea smells like salt.
The sand feels soft.
The sand sounds quiet.
The sand smells salty.

Lorenzo Alfredo Garcia-Jones (6)
Fishponds CE Academy, Fishponds

Winter

W et
I ce
N uts roasting
T oasted toast
E ating warm stuff
R oasting sausages.

Imogen J S Richards (5)
Fishponds CE Academy, Fishponds

Summer

S un
U nder the sun
M oth
M aggot
E vergreen
R ainbow.

Aiza Raheel (6)
Fishponds CE Academy, Fishponds

Summer

S un
U ncold
M oths
M aggots
E vergreen
R ainbows.

Saoirse Linnane (6)

Fishponds CE Academy, Fishponds

The Sea

The sea feels swishy and cold.
It tastes salty.
It sounds weird.

Lucas Tharme (6)
Fishponds CE Academy, Fishponds

The Great Inventor

B ristol-based Clifton, the suspension bridge is his artwork.
R ailway stations and tunnels also built.
U p and down America's coast, SS Great Britain delivered coal.
N ow we admire things he made nearly two hundred years ago.
E ngineer, pioneer that he was.
L iked to work hard to improve travelling.

Who is it?

Answer: Isambard Kingdom Brunel.

Robert Grzegrzolka (5)
Holy Family RC Primary School, Patchway

Seasons

Winter night, winter light,
Everyone is happy, what a good sight.
Summer shine, summer light,
Everyone is happy, everyone is light.
Springtime, spring sight,
All looks wonderful, everything is bright.
Autumn is orange, autumn is bright,
Everything is lovely, everything is light.
So there's winter, spring, summer
and autumn,
And this is the end of seasons time.

Adriana Gomez Serrano (6)
Holy Family RC Primary School, Patchway

All About Nigeria

In Nigeria, we eat plantain because that's
what Nigerian people eat.
In Nigeria, we do Nigeria dances at parties.
In Nigeria, we play football.
In Nigeria, we also wave flags and that
means we want our team to win.
In Nigeria, cocks crow and wake Nigerians
up.
In Nigeria, there are animals in safaris.
We can find lots of animals in peoples
homes.
The rock of Africa.

Dabira Ogundiyan (6)
Holy Family RC Primary School, Patchway

The Cat And The Bat

The cat sat on the mat.
High in the sky, the cat saw a bat.
And guess what?
The bat was wearing a very funny hat.
The bat landed on the mat.
"Hi, cat, I came for a chat."
"I love your hat," said the cat.
"You have a very comfy mat," answered the bat.
"Thank you for a lovely chitchat,"
Smiled the cat and the bat.

Lilyanna Hubay (6)
Holy Family RC Primary School, Patchway

Home Sweet Home

Far away across the oceans,
Far away over the islands,
Many miles away I had to spend,
Many days and nights I keep my strength,
My home is far away,
On a plane, I have to travel,
Many countries I have to cross
Only to find where my real home is.
Sun and beaches always are around,
Mountains and trees sing along
With the wild creatures.

Favio Soares Neves (6)
Holy Family RC Primary School, Patchway

A Unicorn

Unicorns are beautiful and magical.
Unicorns have horns and colourful tails.
Unicorns have smart eyes.
Unicorns are friendly.
I like unicorns because they have colourful hair.
Unicorns and fairies are together.
Fairies can fly and some unicorns can too.
Unicorn magic comes from the horn.

Julia Migdzinska (6)
Holy Family RC Primary School, Patchway

Whatever The Weather

When there is a storm, it is not very warm.
When it's hot, I can play outside.
When there is rain, it can be a real pain.
When there is thunder, it is very loud.
When it's sunny, there are no clouds.
I like summer the best because it is hot and
not cold.

Sophie Daly (6)
Holy Family RC Primary School, Patchway

Gus' OMG Cool Diary

My name is Gustavo, my favourite colour is green,
I have a cool sister, it's really hard to see,
My dad is cool, just like my school.
My mum is fun, just like the sun.

Gustavo Marcante (6)
Holy Family RC Primary School, Patchway

The World

The world is wet.
The world is cold.
The world is beautiful.
The world is old.
The world is hot.
The world is bright.
The world is wonderful
From that window of mine.

Skyla-Zian Ward (6)
Holy Family RC Primary School, Patchway

Summer

In the summer
I can feel the long, green grass blowing in
my face.
I can hear mosquitoes buzzing in my room
and the funny ice cream van's tune.
I can smell the fresh air.
I can see good, clean water.
I can taste ice cream and milkshakes.
Summer makes me playful.

Daisy Duhig (6)
North Cadbury CE Primary School, North Cadbury

Summer

In the summer
I can feel the cold water on the water slide.
I can hear the birds tweeting loudly.
I can smell the fresh ice cream bubbling.
I can see white clouds floating slowly in the sky.
I can taste the creamy chocolate milkshake on a hot day.
Summer makes me happy.

Izzy Hix (7)
North Cadbury CE Primary School, North Cadbury

Summer

In the summer
I can feel the soft wind breathing.
I can hear the mosquitoes flapping around
in the blue sky.
I can smell the nice, fresh air.
I can see the bright green leaves waving on
the trees.
I can taste the cold fresh water.
Summer makes me feel amazing.

Layla Fitzpatrick
North Cadbury CE Primary School, North Cadbury

Summer

In the summer
I can feel the hotness running up my pink
neck.
I can hear the sea swaying and beautiful
birds.
I can smell the banana cake in the oven.
I can see blossom on the trees.
I can taste imaginary gold chocolate.
Summer makes me feel hot.

Lily Austin (6)
North Cadbury CE Primary School, North Cadbury

Summer

In the summer
I can feel the long grass swishing near me.
I can hear the birds singing and tweeting.
I can smell the strawberry milkshakes.
I can see the pretty leaves and trees.
I can taste the delicious creamy ice cream.
Summer makes me playful.

Lola Gray (6)
North Cadbury CE Primary School, North Cadbury

Summer

In the summer
I can feel the cold water splashing on my
chest from my waterslide.
I can hear the noisy flies flying around.
I can smell the delicious sweets.
I can see the bright sun.
I can taste the appetising sausages.
Summer makes me feel free.

Ollie Sweetlove (6)
North Cadbury CE Primary School, North Cadbury

YoungWriters

Summer

In the summer
I can feel the cold ice cream.
I can hear the pesky mosquitoes.
I can smell cakes.
I can see the beautiful blue sky.
I can taste the delicious, creamy chocolate
milkshakes on a hot day.
Summer makes me happy.

Dylan Jack Fred Purdy (5)
North Cadbury CE Primary School, North Cadbury

Summer

In the summer
I can feel grass tickling my feet.
I can hear mosquitoes stinging me.
I can smell chocolate melting in the sun.
I can see blue skies moving.
I can taste chocolate milkshake.
Summer makes me feel excited.

Leo David Stone (7)
North Cadbury CE Primary School, North Cadbury

Summer

In the summer
I can feel the wind breathing on my face
gently.
I can hear the birds flying and tweeting in
the sky beautifully.
I can smell the delicious vanilla and
chocolate ice cream.
I can see the sun shining in the bright sky.

Enya Gregson (7)
North Cadbury CE Primary School, North Cadbury

Summer

In the summer
I can feel the hot sun shining on my face.
I can hear the wild wind whistling.
I can smell raspberries growing.
I can see the warm blue sky.
I can taste the lovely strawberries ripe.
Summer makes me feel happy.

Amalia Katherine Clarke (6)
North Cadbury CE Primary School, North Cadbury

Summer

I can feel the freshly cut grass under my feet.
I can hear the gorgeous birds tweeting in the sky.
I can smell the delicious food from the barbecue.

Finlay Kingshott (6)

North Cadbury CE Primary School, North Cadbury

Gymnastics

G oing to the gym is lots of fun.

Y ou learn new tricks.

M aking it fun for everyone.

N ever had a clue when I was new

A nd now I find it easy to do.

S plits, cartwheels and handstands

T hat's what I love to do.

I sometimes go to

C ompetitions and gymnastics shows too

S o why not join our club, put your nerves
   aside and give it at try.

Lily Hoddinott (8)

St Aldhelm's CE (VA) Primary School, Doulting

Football

F antastic game you might like.

O h my, it's a tie in the final.

O h my, I'm in the final tonight.

T o make sure you do well.

B ut it doesn't matter about winning, it matters about taking part.

A fantastic game you'll love to play.

L ose a few games, win a few games.

L ook up and pass.

Corey Lincoln (8)
St Aldhelm's CE (VA) Primary School, Doulting

A Special Bond

We like to giggle and play
But sometimes he gets in the way.
Cuddles are okay when he's happy to take care
But sometimes he can be a nightmare.
We love each other, like stars shining bright
But sometimes we like to fight.
We are always there for each other.
Who is he?

Answer: My brother.

Oliver Harris (7)
St Aldhelm's CE (VA) Primary School, Doulting

The Football Player

I have two kinds of football boots.
I have one pair of shin pads.
I play for Tottenham.
I am twenty-five years old.
My country is England.
I play football.
I live in London.
I have blonde hair.
Who am I?

Answer: Harry Kane.

Fabio Knott (8)
St Aldhelm's CE (VA) Primary School, Doulting

Grant

G is for Grant because that's my name.

R is for reading because I love it.

A is for answering hard questions.

N is for FortNite because that's my favourite game.

T is for, "That's all folks!"

Grant Jeffery (8)

St Aldhelm's CE (VA) Primary School, Doulting

A Special Pet

I am small, cuddly, warm and fluffy.
I like to nibble toes and chase insects
around the garden.
I like to run, jump and climb.
I have stripy fur and green eyes.
I like to hunt and chase balls.
What am I?

Answer: A cat.

Harry Bassett (8)
St Aldhelm's CE (VA) Primary School, Doulting

I Love Racing

R unning as fast as I can.

A ll the way to the end.

C hecking I'm in the lead.

E njoying it will get me all the way.

S oon I'll cross the finish line.

Sienna Oakman (7)
St Aldhelm's CE (VA) Primary School, Doulting

What Am I?

I am green and turn yellow.
I live in a bunch.
I am shaped like the moon.
Monkeys like to eat me,
But don't slip on my skin!
What am I?

Answer: A banana.

Alfie Beachcroft (8)
St Aldhelm's CE (VA) Primary School, Doulting

Unicorns On Rainbows

I'm small.
I'm fluffy.
I dance on rainbows.
I'm a magic creator.
Fairies ride me.
Who am I?

Answer: A unicorn dancing on rainbows.

Lola Gregory (7)
St Aldhelm's CE (VA) Primary School, Doulting

Flying High

I flew a jet in the sky,
I couldn't take my pet, I wonder why?
At the airport was a marshall,
I had cake, I was quite partial.

Owen Pitman (8)
St Aldhelm's CE (VA) Primary School, Doulting

Ice Cream

I ce creams are cold and delicious
C reamy and soft and the cone is crunchy
E verybody is going up for ice cream

C hildren like ice cream
R eally sunny day
E veryone came to my house for ice cream
A lways have people come to the van for ice cream
M any people like ice cream.

Nikita Fisher (6)
St John's CE Primary School, Midsomer Norton

Ice Cream

I t's a sunny day.
C ornets are my favourite.
E very flavour you can think of!

C hocolate is the best.
R emember to not let your ice cream drip.
E at it all up.
A t the bottom, it tastes the best.
M ake sure the seagulls don't eat your ice cream!

Alicia Hurst (6)
St John's CE Primary School, Midsomer Norton

Ice Cream

I ce creams are tasty on a hot day
C hocolate is my favourite
E verybody likes ice cream in cones.

C old ice creams
R eally sunny day
E veryone likes ice cream
A ll ice cream is freezing
M y favourite is chocolate.

Isla Seymour (6)
St John's CE Primary School, Midsomer Norton

Rainbow

R ain sparkles and drops down into trees.

A bee buzzes around the garden.

I feel happy.

N ice flowers smell like honey.

B elow it is a pot of gold.

O range, blue, red, green and yellow.

W onderful colours.

Isla Miles (6)
St John's CE Primary School, Midsomer Norton

Summer

Summer is boiling.
Summer is going to the beaches.
Summer is ice cream mountains.
Summer is relaxing.
Summer barbecues.
Summer is going to France.
Summer is rain.
Summer is lots of fun.
Summer is going out.
Summer is surfboarding.

Ethan Simcox (6)
St John's CE Primary School, Midsomer Norton

Flowers

F lowers are budding
L ots of different varieties
O range flowers are beautiful
W et, shining petals
E njoy the smells of the flowers
R emember to not pick them
S un makes the flowers grow.

Isaac Brooks (6)

St John's CE Primary School, Midsomer Norton

Holiday

H ot sunny days
O n the beach it's fun
L ollies with my brother
I n the sunshine we have fun
D igging with a bucket and spade
A big beach to play on
Y ellow sun shining down.

Hannah Evans (6)
St John's CE Primary School, Midsomer Norton

Winter

W hen it snows I get excited.

I ce is cold and slippery.

N ice hot chocolate to drink.

T he snow is sparkling in the sun.

E veryone is staying inside.

R ide down on the sledge.

James Parry (6)
St John's CE Primary School, Midsomer Norton

Flower

F eels delicate.

L ooks colourful and pretty.

O range, red and yellow is on flowers.

W hite blossom is on the trees.

E ach bee flies around.

R oses sparkle in the sun.

Freddie Maule (6)

St John's CE Primary School, Midsomer Norton

Spring

S unny flowers look beautiful.
P retty trees sparkle in the rain.
R ainbows are colourful.
I feel amazing.
N ectar smells like honey.
G reen glistening grass.

Sophia Perry (6)
St John's CE Primary School, Midsomer Norton

Beach

B eaches are fun on hot days.

E very flavour of ice cream you can think of.

A big wave is coming.

C hocolate ice cream is the best.

H ot sunny days are great fun.

Taylor Rose Hampson (7)
St John's CE Primary School, Midsomer Norton

Spring

S unny days are beautiful
P oppies are growing.
R ainbows are made by rain and sun.
I feel amazing.
N ectar is sweet.
G o and find some flowers.

Poppy-Lou Tustin (6)
St John's CE Primary School, Midsomer Norton

Summer

Summer is fun.
Summer is fun.
Summer is football.
Summer is going on holidays.
Summer is swimming.
Summer is picnics.
Summer is coming soon.

Joshua Anderson (6)
St John's CE Primary School, Midsomer Norton

Deep Patrol

In the ocean, I might see a beautiful blue angelfish floating along the magnificent ocean floor.
In the ocean, I might see an electric eel whizzing by.
In the ocean, I might touch the beautiful red coral.
In the ocean, I might taste salty water on my red tongue.
In the ocean, I might hear a big blue wave splashing down on the rocks.

Alfie Cochrane (7)

St Nicholas CE Primary School, Henstridge

In The Deep Blue

In the ocean, I might see a beautiful angel fish floating through the salty water.
In the ocean, I might smell a bit of salt in the sea.
In the ocean, I might taste a scary, yummy shark.
In the ocean, I might touch a slippery, smelly fish.
In the ocean, I might hear the swishing coral.

Ronnie Smith (7)
St Nicholas CE Primary School, Henstridge

The Ocean Deep

In the sea, I can smell a scary killer whale.
In the sea, I can taste the salty sea.
In the sea, I can see scary, giant
hammerhead sharks.
In the sea, I can hear the beautiful sound of
the waves.
In the sea, I can touch a beautiful turtle in
the beautiful sea.

Ryan Shearing (7)
St Nicholas CE Primary School, Henstridge

The Whooshing Ocean

In the ocean, I can smell seaweed.
In the ocean, I can taste salty water.
In the ocean, I can hear the whales singing.
In the ocean, I can touch shiny blue fish.
In the ocean, I can feel sharp rocks.
In the ocean, I can see a colourful rainbow
fish.

Archie Craig (7)
St Nicholas CE Primary School, Henstridge

The Ocean Deep

In the ocean, I can touch slippery, slimy
shells.
In the ocean, I can see rainbow, glittery
angelfish floating in the sea.
In the ocean, I can taste salty water.
In the ocean, I can hear blue glittery water.
In the ocean, I can smell salty water.

Izabella Shearer (6)
St Nicholas CE Primary School, Henstridge

The Ocean Deep

I can touch the magical, satisfying coral swaying in the sea.
I can hear the clear popping bubbles of a dolphin wriggling in the sea.
I can smell a mysterious rotten fishy smell coming my way.
I can taste the salty sea everywhere I go.

Amy Cluett (7)
St Nicholas CE Primary School, Henstridge

Sea Creatures

In the sea, I can touch stripy clownfish.
In the sea, I can touch a turtle so big.
In the sea, I can taste the salty sea.
In the sea, I can hear a big wave.
In the sea, I can smell a crab's shell.

Daniel Furlong (6)
St Nicholas CE Primary School, Henstridge

Spash In The Sea

A pretty dolphin.
The salty water for a seahorse.
The shiny water,
The shiny fish scales,
The shiny shark teeth.
A dimmed yellow fish.
The seahorse does a loop-de-loop.
The turtle swims back through.

Ella Frampton
St Nicholas CE Primary School, Henstridge

Sea Patrol

In the ocean, I will taste a good, amazing turtle.
In the ocean, I can smell gorgeous angelfish.
In the ocean, I can see a hammerhead in the ocean.
In the ocean, I can hear scary sharks.

Zachary Peckover (6)
St Nicholas CE Primary School, Henstridge

The Nice Beautiful Ocean

I might smell the nice waves.
I might taste the beautiful ocean.
I might touch the beautiful coral.
I might see a big, scary electric eel.
I might hear the fish sleeping.

Shane Cherrington (6)
St Nicholas CE Primary School, Henstridge

The Ocean

In the ocean, I can see a whale.
In the ocean, I can hear a fish.
In the ocean, I can taste salty water.
In the ocean, I can see fish.
In the ocean, I can feel fish.

Courtney-Mae Read (6)
St Nicholas CE Primary School, Henstridge

The Ocean Deep

In the ocean, I can see fish.
In the ocean, I can hear an eel.
In the ocean, I can feel a shark.
In the ocean, I can see coral.
In the ocean, I can taste the water.

Jessica Squires (6)
St Nicholas CE Primary School, Henstridge

Sea Patrol

In the ocean, I can see beautiful fish.
In the ocean, I can see shiny scales.
In the ocean, I can see squid floating
beneath me.
In the ocean, I can see fish floating.

Finn Jameson (5)
St Nicholas CE Primary School, Henstridge

Under The Ocean Deep

In the ocean, I would hear a blowing whale and some settling weights.
In the ocean, I would see an oily fish and a clownfish.
In the ocean, I would touch a slimy fish.

Kaydie Cherrington (7)

St Nicholas CE Primary School, Henstridge

Grandma

My grandma sounds as gentle as a leaf
falling down from a tree.
My grandma smells like purple lavender.
My grandma feels as soft as a pillow.
My grandma tastes like cake with sprinkles
on.
My grandma looks kind with blue eyes.

Cecily Gasson-Hargreaves (5)
Sunny Hill Preparatory School, Bruton

Ned, My Dog

Ned sounds like a bird screaming when the doorbell goes.
Ned is as black as a bat hanging upside down.
Ned smells like a rat in the sewer.
Ned feels as fluffy as a polar bear.
Ned tastes like pork roast dinners.

Jamie Stean (7)
Sunny Hill Preparatory School, Bruton

The Rocking Robot

My robot sounds like a dragon roaring.
My robot feels as soft as a book cover.
My robot looks like an incredible metal human.
My robot tastes like slippery oil from a car.
My robot smells of screws and magnets.

Isabelle Kettle (6)
Sunny Hill Preparatory School, Bruton

My Cuddly Cat

He sounds like a purring baby, sometimes a
screaming child.
My cuddly cat smells of dead birds.
My cuddly cat looks like a big black ball of
wool.
He feels like a fluffy woolly jumper.
He tastes of furballs.

Tabitha Bayliss (6)
Sunny Hill Preparatory School, Bruton

Stormzee, My Cat

Stormzee sounds like a screeching parrot.
Stormzee feels soft and smooth like a
teddy bear.
Stormzee smells like tuna fish.
Stormzee looks like a fluffy white cloud.
Stormzee tastes like fish pie.

Nina Markussdottir (5)

Sunny Hill Preparatory School, Bruton

Scruffy

Scruffy looks like an orangey-brown bear.
Scruffy feels as precious as an old snow
globe.
Scruffy sounds like the countryside.
Scruffy tastes like chocolate bars.
Scruffy smells like home.

Rose Ward (6)

Sunny Hill Preparatory School, Bruton

Matilda Rabbit

My rabbit is quiet as a tiny mouse.
My rabbit looks like Peter Rabbit without a
jacket.
My rabbit smells like dry straw.
My rabbit feels like a lion's mane.

Rose Turner (5)
Sunny Hill Preparatory School, Bruton

Summer Superstar

When the bright sun is out,
I go into the hot sun
And have particular playtime,
Eat ice cream and have a good time.
Oh, how I adore those days in the sun
And I will be the one and only to adore
those days.
I'm always eager to go out and for good
reason, I never shout.
I love those days.
Some people scream but I never scream,
I adore those days...
Properly!

Coco Green (6)
The Dolphin School, Bristol

Leopard

L eaps as high as a great giraffe.

E legant and active.

O nly it cares for its tiny and untamed cub.

P olite and graceful like an elephant.

A lways has its roar ready.

R oars like a lion but a bit sweeter and quieter.

D rinks from a little bowl made from the ground.

Martha Eldred (7)

The Dolphin School, Bristol

What Are They?

They're fast, fearless animals.
They have sharp teeth, long tails, black
spots, round ears and orange fur.
They're actually big cats.
They're talented and brave.
They're as fast as a firework.
They have a lot of energy.
What are they?

Answer: Cheetahs.

Eliza Jane Postema (7)
The Dolphin School, Bristol

Lizards

L et me tell you about lizards.

I t's fun as a pet.

Z igzagging all around.

A ctually sometimes good to keep.

R arely ever red.

D on't let them bite!

S ome are cute, some are scary, but all are really scaly.

Farris Shandis (7)
The Dolphin School, Bristol

Butterfly

B it bigger than a bee.

U nder the hot sun.

T raced wings.

T raced wings.

E ven near flowers.

R ed flowers, my favourite.

F lying, flying.

L ovely flowers.

Y ou are my friend.

Aki Maxwell (7)

The Dolphin School, Bristol

Summer

The hot warm sun shining
A circle in the sky
Next to the blue sky that we know
Then wet, wet, wet
Sweat, sweat, sweat
All over our body
Because summer, summer is here
Also glimmering beautiful summer.

Alina Kabir (7)
The Dolphin School, Bristol

Snake

S lithering slower than a slug.

N ice pattern on the back.

A n insect is so small that it can chase them as fast as a flash.

K arate kicking fast.

E ating insects on the floor.

Ashley-Joseph Dymond-Bailey (7)
The Dolphin School, Bristol

Unicorn Sparkle

Unicorns shine bright in the sky.
Glowing like Christmas Day.
Party starts every day.
Party dresses have glitter on.
Every day we have fun.
Santa came at Christmas.
Unicorns are lazy.

Eshaal Fatima Shakeel (7)
The Dolphin School, Bristol

Who Am I?

I live with seven dwarfs.
I have hair as black as ebony.
I used to live with my stepmother but I got
lost in the woods.
Who am I?

Answer: Snow White.

Leen Elmouiz Siddeg Hessien (6)
The Dolphin School, Bristol

Zebra

Z ebras are cute and fluffy.
E ven they have babies.
B abies are smart and good.
R unning and drinking
A nd drinking from their mums.

Umamah Hassan (7)
The Dolphin School, Bristol

Riddle

I am scared of dogs.
I am bright orange and stripy.
I eat tuna.
I drink milk.
I have fur.
I like to chase mice.
What am I?

Answer: A cat.

Ahmed Mohamed (7)
The Dolphin School, Bristol

Owl

O n top of the world with glowing owl eyes.
W ith wings of sparkle that flow like blue
  fire.
L ike an aeroplane making *tweet, tweet,*
  twoo sounds.

Suhana Gill (7)
The Dolphin School, Bristol

Summer

Summer, don't go away when it is the end
of the day
The light from the sun glimmers on the sea
What a beautiful season you are
I will make sure you stay with me.

Isra Ismail (7)
The Dolphin School, Bristol

A Riddle You'll Never Forget

I love to make people happy.
I like to see children laugh
And to see children dancing in the roses.
Who am I?

Answer: Summer.

Annaliese Smith (7)
The Dolphin School, Bristol

Monkey

Monkeys like to hug.
Monkeys like to play.
Monkeys like to go swimming with the
children.
Monkeys have soft fur.
Monkeys are hungry.

Myar Khalil
The Dolphin School, Bristol

I Am White!

I am white.
I am light to carry.
I am pretty in the night.
I am pretty in the light.
What am I?

Answer: A swan.

Amelie Papworth Jory (7)
The Dolphin School, Bristol

Lion

L azy like a sloth.
I ndestructible sharp claws.
O verly fluffy mane.
N ever get scared.

Zakoni Barrington Alcott-Kennett (7)
The Dolphin School, Bristol

A Speedy Animal

I like to eat meat.
I live in a hot country.
I have great eyesight.
What am I?

Answer: A cheetah.

Nehal Sunu (6)
The Dolphin School, Bristol

Frogs In Rain

Frogs like puddles with rain.
Frogs like water and paddling pools.
Frogs like mud and hopping around.

Owen Taylor (7)
The Dolphin School, Bristol

Frogs

Frogs are slimy and jumpy.
Frogs are green and eat bugs.
Frogs are horrible and live in puddles.

Kenneth Oommen Panicker (7)
The Dolphin School, Bristol